Assassin's Apprentice

Assassin's Apprentice

Written by
Robin Hobb and Jody Houser

Script by
Jody Houser

Illustrated by
Ryan Kelly

Color Art by
Jordie Bellaire

Letters by
Hassan Otsmane-Elhaou

Cover Art by
Anna Steinbauer

Assassin's Apprentice *Created by Robin Hobb*

HARPER
Voyager

President and Publisher
Mike Richardson

Editor
Brett Israel

Assistant Editor
Sanjay Dharawat

Digital Art Technician
Samantha Hummer

Collection Designer
Kristofer McRae

ASSASSIN'S APPRENTICE
Copyright © 2023 by Robin Hobb. Based on the novel *Assassin's Apprentice*, copyright © 1995 by Robin Hobb. Dark Horse Books® and the Dark Horse logo are registered trademarks of Dark Horse Comics LLC. All rights reserved. Dark Horse is part of Embracer Group.

Harper*Voyager* an imprint of HarperCollins*Publishers* Ltd
1 London Bridge Street, London, SE1 9GF

www.harpercollins.co.uk

HarperCollinsPublishers
Macken House, 39/40 Mayor Street Upper,
Dublin 1, D01 C9W8, Ireland

First published in Great Britain by HarperCollinsPublishers 2023

1

Written by Robin Hobb and Jody Houser; script by Jody Houser; illustrated by Ryan Kelly; color art by Jordie Bellaire; letters by Hassan Otsmane-Elhaou; cover art by Anna Steinbauer.

A catalogue record for this book is available from the British Library.

ISBN: 978-0-00-868248-4

Printed and bound in the U.K. by Bell & Bain Ltd.

Chapter One

A History of the Six Duchies is of necessity a history of its ruling family, the Farseers.

Of the first real King, little more than his name and some extravagant legends remain.

Taker his name was, quite simply, and perhaps with that naming began the tradition...

...that daughters and sons of his lineage would be given names that would shape their lives and beings.

FATHER, PLEASE.

Folk beliefs claim that such names were sealed to the newborn babes by magic.

FATHER!

That these royal offspring were incapable of betraying the virtues whose names they bore.

PLEASE, I *BEG* YOU!

RAP RAP

Passed through fire and plunged through salt-water and offered to the winds of the air.

Thus were names sealed to these chosen children.

So we are told.

But history shows us this was not always sufficient to bind a child to the virtue that named it...

I'VE BROUGHT THE BOY TO YOU.

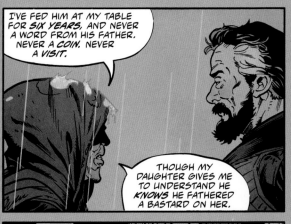

I'VE FED HIM AT MY TABLE FOR *SIX YEARS*, AND NEVER A WORD FROM HIS FATHER. NEVER A *COIN*. NEVER A *VISIT*.

THOUGH MY DAUGHTER GIVES ME TO UNDERSTAND HE *KNOWS* HE FATHERED A BASTARD ON HER.

I'LL NOT FEED HIM ANY LONGER. I'VE *ENOUGH* TO TEND TO OF MY OWN. LET HIM BE FED BY HIM WHAT GOT HIM. YOU TAKE HIM, AND GIVE HIM TO HIS FATHER.

WHOSE GET?

PRINCE *CHIVALRY'S*. HIM WHAT'S KING-IN-WAITING.

BE GLAD HE MANAGED TO FATHER *ONE* CHILD, SOME-WHERE.

WELL, JASON? WHAT'S THIS?

AN OLD PLOWMAN LEFT HIM, PRINCE VERITY, SIR.

SAYS IT'S *PRINCE CHIVALRY'S* BASTID, SIR.

BE DAMNED...

BOY *DOES* HAVE CHIV'S LOOK TO HIM, DOESN'T HE? FRUITFUL EDA.

WHO'D HAVE BELIEVED IT OF MY *ILLUSTRIOUS* AND *VIRTUOUS* BROTHER?

DAMN, YES. SEVEN YEARS AGO, THE FIRST YEAR THE CHYURDA TRIED TO CLOSE THE PASS.

CHIVALRY WAS UP THIS WAY FOR THREE, FOUR MONTHS. CHIVYING THEM INTO OPENING IT TO US.

LOOKS LIKE IT WASN'T THE *ONLY* THING HE CHIVIED OPEN.

WHO'S THE MOTHER?

DON'T KNOW, SIR. THERE WAS ONLY THE OLD PLOWMAN ON THE DOOR-STEP.

HERE, BOY. WHAT DO THEY CALL YOU?

"BOY."

WELL. SOME-THING'S GOT TO BE DONE WITH HIM, AT LEAST UNTIL CHIV GETS BACK.

SEE THE BOY'S FED AND BEDDED FOR TONIGHT. I'LL GIVE THIS MORE THOUGHT TOMORROW.

CAN'T HAVE ROYAL BASTARDS CLUTTERING UP THE COUNTRYSIDE.

SIR.

DUNK

SOGGY LITTLE PUP, YOU.

HERE, BURRICH. THIS PUP'S FOR YOU, NOW.

WHAT'S THIS?

HE'S YOURS TO WATCH OVER. PRINCE VERITY SAYS SO.

WHY?

YOU'RE CHIVALRY'S MAN, AIN'T YOU? CARE FOR HIS HORSE, HIS HOUNDS, HIS HAWKS?

SO, YOU GOT HIS LITTLE BASTID, AT LEAST UNTIL CHIVALRY GETS BACK AND DOES OTHERWISE WITH HIM.

CHIVALRY'S BASTARD?

SO SAID THE OLD PLOWMAN WHAT LEFT HIM HERE.

SAID CHIVALRY OUGHT TO BE GLAD HE'D SEEDED ONE CHILD, SOMEWHERE.

THAT HE SHOULD FEED AND CARE FOR HIM HIMSELF NOW.

IF MY MASTER HAS NO HEIR, 'TIS *EDA'S WILL*, AND NO FAULT OF HIS MANHOOD.

THE LADY PATIENCE HAS *ALWAYS* BEEN DELICATE.

EVEN SO, EVEN SO.

AND THERE SITS THE VERY PROOF THAT THERE'S NOWT WRONG WITH HIM AS A MAN.

AS IS ALL I WAS SAYING, THAT'S ALL.

IT'S A THING THAT WILL TRY HER LADY'S WILL TO THE EDGE OF HER VERY NAME.

WHO'D CHIVALRY GET HIM ON?

I'D SAY IT WAS *PRINCE CHIVALRY'S* BUSINESS WHO THE MOTHER WAS.

AND *NOT FOR* KITCHEN TALK.

EVEN SO, EVEN SO.

BOY DON'T HAVE A NAME.

JUST GOES BY "BOY."

WELL, IF I KNOW YOUR FATHER, HE'LL FACE UP TO IT SQUARE AND DO WHAT'S RIGHT.

BUT EDA ONLY *KNOWS* WHAT HE'LL THINK IS THE RIGHT THING TO DO. PROBABLY WHATEVER HURTS THE *MOST.*

HAD ENOUGH TO EAT?

COME ON, THEN, FITZ.

HAWKS ARE DOWN AT THE FAR END.

I remember that first night well.

HERE. THIS'LL DO FOR NOW. I'M JIGGED IF I KNOW WHAT *ELSE* TO DO WITH YOU.

NOSY, YOU JUST MOVE OVER AND MAKE THIS BOY A PLACE IN THE STRAW.

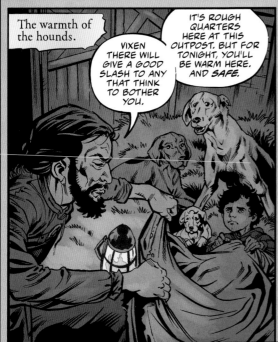

The warmth of the hounds.

VIXEN THERE WILL GIVE A GOOD SLASH TO ANY THAT THINK TO BOTHER YOU.

IT'S ROUGH QUARTERS HERE AT THIS OUTPOST. BUT FOR TONIGHT, YOU'LL BE WARM HERE. AND *SAFE*.

HORSE, HOUND, AND HAWK, CHIVALRY. I'VE MINDED THEM ALL FOR YOU FOR MANY A YEAR, AND MINDED THEM *WELL*.

BUT THIS BY-BLOW OF YOURS, WELL... WHAT TO *DO* WITH HIM IS *BEYOND* ME.

The prickling straw.

YAP
YAP

NOW YOU'VE WAKENED HIM.

SO? HE'LL GO BACK TO SLEEP AS SOON AS WE LEAVE.

DAMN HIM, HE HAS HIS FATHER'S EYES AS WELL. I SWEAR, I'D HAVE KNOWN HIS BLOOD ANYWHERE.

THERE'LL BE NO DENYING IT TO ANY THAT SEE HIM.

BUT HAVE NEITHER YOU NOR BURRICH THE SENSE OF A FLEA?

BASTARD OR NOT, YOU DON'T STABLE A CHILD AMONG BEASTS.

REGAL, I HAD GIVEN IT NO THOUGHT. WHAT DO I KNOW OF CHILDREN?

I TURNED HIM OVER TO BURRICH. HE IS CHIVALRY'S MAN, AND AS SUCH HE'S CARED FOR.

I MEANT NO DISRESPECT TO THE BLOOD, SIR. I SAW TO THE BOY AS I THOUGHT BEST.

HE SEEMS SMALL TO HAVE A PALLET IN THE GUARDROOM, WITH FIGHTS AND DRINKING AND NOISE OF THE MEN.

BEDDED HERE, HE HAS QUIET, AND THE PUP HAS TAKEN TO HIM.

AND WITH MY VIXEN TO WATCH OVER HIM AT NIGHT, NO ONE COULD DO HIM HARM.

IT'S FINE, BURRICH, IT'S FINE. I LEFT IT TO YOU, AND I DON'T FIND FAULT WITH IT.

IT'S BETTER THAN A LOT OF CHILDREN HAVE IN THIS VILLAGE, EDA KNOWS. FOR HERE, FOR NOW, IT'S FINE.

IT WILL HAVE TO BE DIFFERENT WHEN HE COMES BACK TO BUCKKEEP.

THEN OUR FATHER WISHES HIM TO RETURN WITH US TO BUCKKEEP?

OUR FATHER DOES. MY MOTHER DOES NOT.

AND *THIS* WILL MAKE THE PEOPLE LIKE HIM MORE? SUPPORT HIS FUTURE KINGSHIP MORE?

THAT HE FATHERED A CHILD ON SOME... *WILD WOMAN* BEFORE HE MARRIED HIS QUEEN?

SO THE KING SEEMS TO THINK. I SUSPECT CHIVALRY WILL FEEL *DIFFERENTLY* ABOUT USING HIS BASTARD IN SUCH A WAY.

ESPECIALLY AS IT REGARDS DEAR PATIENCE.

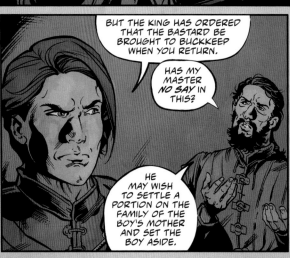

BUT THE KING HAS ORDERED THAT THE BASTARD BE BROUGHT TO BUCKKEEP WHEN YOU RETURN.

HAS MY MASTER *NO SAY* IN THIS?

HE MAY WISH TO SETTLE A PORTION ON THE FAMILY OF THE BOY'S MOTHER AND SET THE BOY ASIDE.

SURELY FOR THE SAKE OF MY LADY PATIENCE'S SENSIBILITIES, HE SHOULD BE ALLOWED THAT DISCRETION.

THE TIME FOR DISCRETION WAS *BEFORE* HE ROLLED THE WENCH.

THE LADY PATIENCE IS NOT THE FIRST WOMAN TO HAVE TO FACE HER *HUSBAND'S* BASTARD.

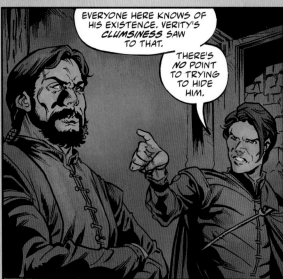

EVERYONE HERE KNOWS OF HIS EXISTENCE. VERITY'S *CLUMSINESS* SAW TO THAT.

THERE'S *NO POINT* TO TRYING TO HIDE HIM.

AND AS FAR AS A ROYAL BASTARD IS CONCERNED, *NONE* OF US CAN AFFORD TO HAVE SUCH SENSIBILITIES, BURRICH.

TO LEAVE SUCH A BOY IN A PLACE LIKE THIS IS LIKE LEAVING A *WEAPON* HOVERING OVER THE KING'S *THROAT.*

SURELY EVEN A *HOUNDSMAN* CAN SEE THAT.

afraid afraid afraid afraid

AND EVEN IF *YOU* CAN'T, YOUR *MASTER* WILL.

GR RR

I'D THOUGHT YOUR BEASTS TO BE *BETTER TRAINED,* BURRICH.

If all I had ever done was be born and discovered, I would have left a mark across all the land for all time.

I was Chivalry's monumental failure. He preceded us home to Buckkeep, where he abdicated his claim to the throne.

He and Lady Patience were gone from court well before we arrived.

Prince Verity became King-in-Waiting and Prince Regal moved up a notch in the line of succession.

And so I went to Buckkeep, sole child and bastard of a man I'd never know.

Brought to grow up fatherless and motherless in a court where all recognized me as a catalyst.

And a catalyst I would become...

Chapter Two

There are many legends about Taker, the first Outislander to claim Buckkeep as the First Duchy.

The founder of the royal line.

One is that the raiding voyage he was on was his first and only foray out from whatever cold harsh island bore him.

It is said that upon seeing the timbered fortifications of Buckkeep…

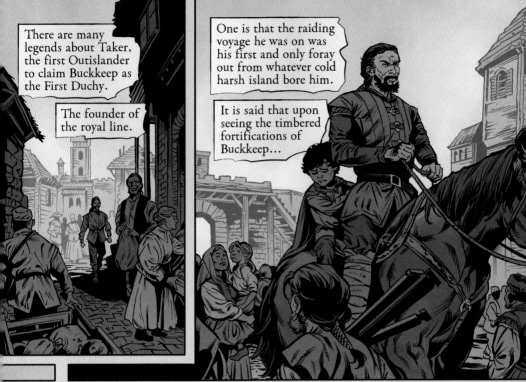

Taker had announced, "If there's a fire and a meal there, I shan't be leaving again."

And there was, and he didn't.

The ruling house of the Six Duchies, the Farseers, were descended from those Outislanders.

Their blood ran strong in the royal lines, producing children with black hair and dark eyes and muscled, stocky limbs.

And with those attributes went a predilection for the Skill…

…and all the dangers and weaknesses inherent in such blood.

I had my share of that heritage too.

HERE, YOU, COB.

TAKE YOUNG FITZ THERE TO THE KITCHENS AND SEE THAT HE'S FED.

ARE YOU HUNGRY, THEN, FITZ?

SHALL WE GO FIND YOU A BITE?

COME ALONG NOW, *THERE'S* SOME GOOD FELLOWS.

smell

food

good

PLACE IS *PACKED.* EVERYONE'S GETTING READY FOR THE WELCOMING FEAST TONIGHT, FOR VERITY AND REGAL.

ANYONE WHO'S *ANYONE* HAS COME INTO BUCKKEEP FOR IT; WORD SPREAD *FAST* ABOUT CHIVALRY DUCKING OUT ON THE KINGSHIP--

LOOK, JUST WAIT HER I'LL SLIP IN AND BRIN SOMETHING OUT FOR YOU.

LESS CHANCE OF ME GETTING STEPPED ON, OR *CAUGHT.*

NOW *STAY.*

YOU THE *BASTID,* HEY?

STIFF-AS-A-STICK CHIVALRY'S *BY BLOW.* LOOKS A FAIR BIT LIKE HIM.

WHO'S YOUR MOTHER?

WHAT'S YOUR NAME THEN, BOY?

just a pup *cannot defend* *have mercy*

I HEARD HE AIN'T *GOT* NO NAME. NO HIGHFLOWN ROYAL *NAME* TO SHAPE HIM.

NOR EVEN A *COTTAGE NAME* TO SCOLD HIM BY. THAT *RIGHT,* BOY? YOU GOT A NAME?

I *SAID,* YOU GOT A *NAME,* BOY?

afraid

NO.

NO!

THERE YOU ARE. COME ALONG THEN.

I *LIED* TO MY KING TODAY FOR YOU. *FIRST TIME* EVER IN MY LIFE I'VE DONE THAT.

APPEARS AS IF CHIVALRY'S FALL FROM GRACE WILL TAKE *ME* DOWN AS WELL.

TOLD SHREWD YOU WERE SOUND ASLEEP, EXHAUSTED FROM THE JOURNEY.

HE WAS *NOT* PLEASED TO WAIT TO SEE YOU.

LUCKILY FOR US, HE HAD *WEIGHTIER* THINGS TO HANDLE. CHIVALRY'S ABDICATION HAS UPSET A LOT OF LORDS.

NOW, ARE YOU HURT? DID ANYONE ROUGH YOU UP?

GUESS YOU GOT A TASTE OF IT TODAY...

"...I SHOULD HAVE *KNOWN* THERE WOULD BE THOSE WOULD BLAME ALL THE STIR ON YOU."

SOWING THE NEIGHBOR'S FIELDS? QUITE THE ACT OF *CHIVALRY.*

HAHA HAHA HA!

HAHAHA HAHA!

LOOK OUT, NOSE-BLEED!

YOU GOT HER, DIRK!

MISSED AGAIN.

SLOWER THAN AN OLD DRUNK, YOU ARE!

HA HAHA!

BOOOO!

SHUT HER MOUTH!

HEY, WHO'S THAT?

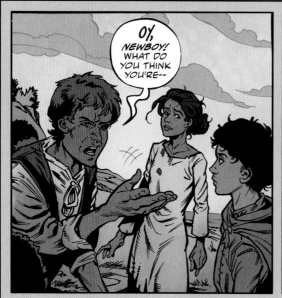

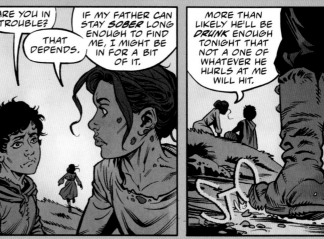

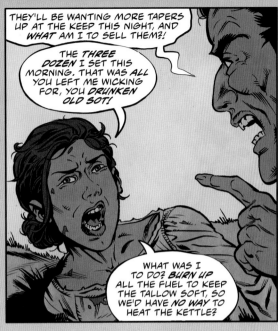

PAPA? PAPA, ARE YOU ALL RIGHT?

PLEASE, DON'T DIE! I'M *SORRY* I'M SUCH A WICKED GIRL!

I'LL BE GOOD! I *PROMISE* I'LL BE GOOD! *DON'T DIE!*

HE...HE WAS GOING TO *KILL* YOU.

NO, NEWBOY. HE HITS ME A *BIT,* WHEN I AM BAD. BUT HE'D *NEVER* KILL ME.

AND WHEN HE IS SOBER AND NOT SICK, HE CRIES ABOUT IT AND BEGS ME NOT BE TOO BAD AND MAKE HIM ANGRY.

I SHOULD TAKE *MORE* CARE NOT TO ANGER HIM.

UHHH...

Having found the town and the beggar children once, they drew me like a magnet every day afterward.

The town became the world to me, with the keep a place I went to sleep.

It was summer, a wonderful time in a port town.

I learned how a quick-footed child might earn three or even five pence a day running messages.

I learned of human nature.

I became a quick judge of who would actually pay the promised penny for a message delivered...

...and who would just laugh at me when I came to collect. Or **worse**.

I knew which baker could be begged from, and which shops were easiest to thieve from.

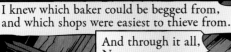

And through it all, Nosy was at my side, so bonded to me now that I seldom separated my mind from his.

I used his nose, his eyes, and his jaws as freely as my own, and never thought it the least bit strange.

But one fine day, with the sun riding a sky bluer than the sea, my good fortune came at last to an end...

HEY!

HM.

STINKING LITTLE THIEF--

HE'S MY CHARGE. I'LL SEE THEY'RE PAID FOR.

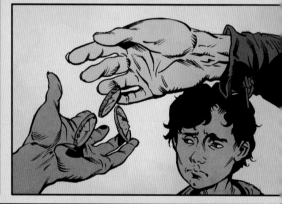

GET HOME. NOW.

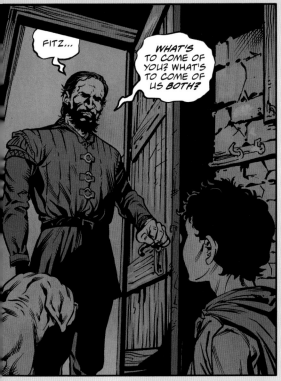

FITZ...

WHAT'S TO COME OF YOU? WHAT'S TO COME OF US *BOTH*?

RUNNING WITH *BEGGAR THIEVES* IN THE STREETS, WITH THE *BLOOD OF KINGS* IN YOUR VEINS. PACKING UP LIKE ANIMALS.

COME HERE, THEN.

COME *HERE*, BOY.

trouble trouble trouble scared? trouble

NO...

KNOW WHAT THIS IS, BOY?

IT'S A DOG WHIP.

IT'S A *TEACHING DEVICE* FOR WHEN YOU GET A PUP THAT WON'T MIND.

A FEW SHARP LASHES FROM THIS, AND THE PUP *LEARNS* TO *LISTEN* AND OBEY THE FIRST TIME.

JUST A FEW *SHARP CUTS* IS ALL IT TAKES.

hurt

pain

beating

scared

OH EDA. I *SUSPECTED* WHEN I SAW YOU RUNNING TOGETHER, BUT *DAMN EL'S EYES,* I DIDN'T WANT TO BE *RIGHT.*

I'VE *NEVER* HIT A PUP WITH THAT DAMN THING IN MY LIFE. NOSY HAD *NO REASON* TO FEAR IT.

NOT UNLESS YOU'D BEEN *SHARING MINDS* WITH HIM.

FITZ, THIS IS *WRONG*. IT'S *VERY BAD*, WHAT YOU'VE BEEN DOING WITH THIS PUP. IT'S *UNNATURAL*.

IT'S WORSE THAN *STEALING* OR *LYING*. IT MAKES A MAN LESS THAN A MAN. AND BOY, YOU'RE OF THE *ROYAL BLOOD*.

BASTARD OR NOT, YOU'RE *CHIVALRY'S SON*, OF THE *OLD LINE*. AND THIS THING YOU'RE DOING IS NOT *WORTHY* OF YOU.

NOW *TALK TO ME*. *WHO* TAUGHT YOU TO DO THIS?

DO WHAT?

YOU *KNOW* WHAT I MEAN. WHO TAUGHT YOU TO BE WITH THE DOG, IN *HIS MIND?*

SEEING THINGS WITH HIM. LETTING *HIM* SEE WITH YOU. *TELLING* EACH OTHER THINGS.

NO ONE. IT JUST... *HAPPENED*.

YOU DON'T SPEAK LIKE A CHILD. BUT I'VE *HEARD* THAT WAS THE WAY OF IT, WITH THOSE WHO HAD THE *OLD WIT*.

THAT THEY WERE NEVER *TRULY* CHILDREN. THEY ALWAYS KNEW *TOO MUCH*, AND AS THEY GOT OLDER, THEY KNEW EVEN MORE.

THAT WAS WHY IT WAS NEVER ACCOUNTED A CRIME, IN THE OLD DAYS, TO *HUNT* THEM DOWN AND *BURN* THEM.

DO YOU UNDER-STAND WHAT I'M TELLING YOU, FITZ?

NO.

BUT I'M *TRYING*.

WHAT IS THE OLD WIT?

THE *OLD WIT*, IT'S THE POWER OF THE *BEAST BLOOD*, JUST AS THE *SKILL* COMES FROM THE *LINE OF KINGS*.

IT STARTS OUT LIKE A BLESSING, GIVING YOU THE TONGUES OF THE ANIMALS. BUT THEN... IT *SEIZES* YOU. DRAWS YOU *DOWN*.

"IT *SHUTS DOWN* YOUR THOUGHTS. MAKES YOU A *BEAST*, SUCH THAT NONE COULD LOOK ON YOU AND THINK YOU HAD *EVER* BEEN A MAN.

"THERE'S SOME AS SAY A MAN TAKES ON THE *SHAPE* OF A BEAST, BUT KILLS WITH A *MAN'S PASSION* RATHER THAN A BEAST'S *SIMPLE HUNGER*."

IS THAT WHAT YOU WAN... FITZ? TO TAKE THE BLOO... OF KINGS THAT'S IN YOU... AND *DROWN* IT IN THE BLOOD OF THE WILD HUNT?

TO BE AS A *BEAST AMONG BEASTS*, SIMPLY FOR THE SAKE OF THE KNOWLEDGE IT BRINGS YOU?

I... DO NOT KNOW.

I TELL YOU WHERE IT WILL LEAD, AND YOU SAY *YOU DON'T KNOW?*

IF CHIVALRY WILL NOT HAVE ME *WITH* HIM, I'LL AT LEAST SEE THAT HIS SON GROWS UP A *MAN*, AND NOT A *WOLF*.

I'LL DO IT IF IT *KILLS* THE BOTH OF US!

scared

take

hurt

no

NO!

helphelphelp

oooWoooooo

"HE'S GONE. THE *PUP'S* GONE."

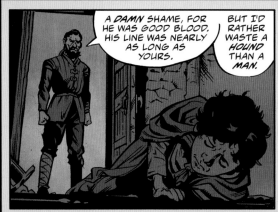

A *DAMN* SHAME, FOR HE WAS GOOD BLOOD. HIS LINE WAS NEARLY AS LONG AS YOURS.

BUT I'D RATHER WASTE A *HOUND* THAN A *MAN.*

LET GO OF LONGING AFTER HIM.

IT HURTS *LESS,* THAT WAY.

...and gradually, Burrich relaxed his watch on me.

KRNCH
KRNCH

YOU *SEE*, REGAL?

IT IS AS I WAS TELLING YOU.

AN OPPORTUNITY PRESENTS ITSELF, AND SOMEONE *SEIZES* IT.

OFTEN SOMEONE YOUNG, OR SOMEONE DRIVEN BY THE *ENERGIES* AND *HUNGERS* OF YOUTH.

ROYALTY HAS *NO* LEISURE TO IGNORE SUCH OPPORTUNITIES.

OR TO LET THEM BE CREATED FOR *OTHERS.*

LOOK AT HIM, REGAL.

WHAT WILL YOU MAKE OF HIM?

HIM? IT'S THE FITZ. CHIVALRY'S *BASTARD*.

SNEAKING AND THIEVING AS ALWAYS.

FOOL.

ARE YOUR EARS STOPPED WITH WAX? DO YOU HEAR *NOTHING* I SAY?

I ASKED YOU, NOT WHAT *DO* YOU MAKE OF HIM...

...BUT WHAT *WILL* YOU MAKE OF HIM?

THERE HE STANDS, *YOUNG, STRONG,* AND *RESOURCEFUL.*

HIS LINES ARE EVERY BIT AS ROYAL AS *YOURS,* FOR ALL THAT HE WAS BORN ON THE *WRONG SIDE* OF THE SHEETS.

SO *WHAT* WILL YOU MAKE OF HIM? A *TOOL?* A *WEAPON?* A *COMRADE?* AN *ENEMY?*

OR WILL YOU LEAVE HIM LYING ABOUT, FOR SOMEONE *ELSE* TO TAKE UP AND USE *AGAINST* YOU?

THE **BASTARD**?

HE'S ONLY A CHILD.

TODAY. THIS MORNING AND **NOW** HE IS A CHILD. WHEN **NEXT** YOU TURN AROUND, HE WILL BE A MAN.

AND THEN IT WILL BE TOO LATE FOR YOU TO MAKE **ANYTHING** OF HIM.

"YOU **COULD** FIND YOURSELF FACING A DISCONTENTED BASTARD.

"ONE WHO MAY BE PERSUADED TO BECOME A **PRETENDER** TO THE THRONE.

"BUT TAKE HIM **NOW**, REGAL, AND **SHAPE** HIM, AND A DECADE HENCE, YOU WILL COMMAND HIS **LOYALTY**.

"HE WILL BE A HENCHMAN, UNITED TO THE FAMILY BY **SPIRIT** AS WELL AS **BLOOD**."

PUT A SIGNET RING ON HIS HAND AND YOU HAVE CREATED A **DIPLOMAT** NO FOREIGN RULER WILL **DARE** TURN AWAY.

HE MAY **SAFELY** BE SENT WHERE A PRINCE OF THE BLOOD MAY NOT BE **RISKED**.

IMAGE THE USES FOR ONE WHO *IS* AND YET *IS NOT* OF THE ROYAL BLOODLINE.

HOSTAGE EXCHANGES. MARITAL ALLIANCES. QUIET WORK. THE DIPLOMACY OF WORDS OR THE KNIFE.

YOU SPEAK OF THESE THINGS *IN FRONT* OF THE BOY.

OF USING HIM, AS A *TOOL*, OR A *WEAPON*.

YOU THINK HE WILL NOT *REMEMBER* YOUR WORDS WHEN HE IS GROWN?

HA HA HA!

REMEMBER THEM? OF COURSE HE WILL. I COUNT ON IT.

LOOK AT HIS EYES, REGAL. THERE IS *INTELLIGENCE* THERE, AND POSSIBLY POTENTIAL SKILL.

I'D BE A *FOOL* TO LIE TO HIM.

STUPIDER STILL TO LEAVE HIS MIND FALLOW FOR WHATEVER SEEDS *OTHERS* MIGHT PLANT THERE.

ISN'T IT SO, BOY?

...YES, SIR.

The original source of the Skill will probably remain forever shrouded in mystery.

COME HERE.

Certainly a penchant for it runs remarkably strong within the royal family.

And yet it is not solely confined to the King's household.

It is interesting to note that the Outislanders seem to have no predilection for the Skill.

Nor the folk descended solely from the original inhabitants of the Six Duchies.

There does seem to be some truth to the folk saying...

NOW...

"When the sea blood flows with the blood of the plains, the Skill will blossom."

...YOU ARE *MINE*.

I WILL *KEEP* YOU, AND I WILL KEEP YOU *WELL*.

IF ANY EVER SEEKS TO TURN YOU AGAINST ME BY OFFERING YOU *MORE*...

...THEN *COME* TO ME, AND *TELL ME* OF THE OFFER, I SHALL *MEET* IT.

YOU WILL *NEVER* FIND ME A STINGY MAN, NOR BE ABLE TO CITE ILL USE AS A REASON FOR TREASON AGAINST ME.

DO YOU *BELIEVE* ME, BOY?

YES, SIR.

GOOD. I WILL BE ISSUING SOME *COMMANDS* REGARDING YOU. SEE THAT YOU GO ALONG WITH THEM.

IF ANY SEEM STRANGE TO YOU, SPEAK TO *BURRICH.* OR TO *MYSELF.*

SIMPLY COME TO THE DOOR OF MY CHAMBER, AND SHOW THAT PIN.

YOU'LL BE ADMITTED.

YES, SIR.

It was my first experience of the Skill at the hands of a master.

AH.

When he turned away from me, a chill went over me, as if I had suddenly shed a cloak.

YOU DON'T APPROVE, *DO YOU,* REGAL?

MY KING MAY DO *WHATEVER* HE WISHES.

THAT IS *NOT* WHAT I ASKED YOU.

MY MOTHER, THE QUEEN, WILL CERTAINLY *NOT* APPROVE.

FAVORING THE BOY WILL *ONLY* MAKE IT APPEAR YOU RECOGNIZE HIM. IT WILL GIVE HIM IDEAS, AND OTHERS.

MY *MOTHER--*

HAS NOT AGREED WITH ME, NOR BEEN PLEASED WITH ME, FOR *SOME YEARS.*

I SCARCELY NOTICE IT ANYMORE, REGAL.

"SHE WILL FLAP AND SQUAWK AND TELL ME *AGAIN* THAT SHE WOULD RETURN TO FARROW, TO BE DUCHESS THERE.

"AND IF VERY ANGRY, SHE WILL THREATEN THAT IF SHE DID, TILTH AND FARROW WOULD RISE UP IN *REBELLION.*"

THAT THEY WILL BECOME A *SEPARATE* KINGDOM, WITH HER AS THE QUEEN.

AND I AS *KING* AFTER HER!

YES, I THOUGHT SHE HAD PLANTED SUCH FESTERING TREASON IN YOUR MIND. *LISTEN,* BOY.

SHE MAY SCOLD AND FLING CROCKERY AT THE SERVANTS, BUT SHE WILL *NEVER* DO MORE THAN THAT.

BECAUSE SHE **KNOWS** IT IS BETTER TO BE QUEEN OF A PEACEFUL KINGDOM THAN DUCHESS OF A DUCHY IN REBELLION.

HER AMBITIONS HAVE **ALWAYS** EXCEEDED HER ABILITIES.

IN ROYALTY, THAT IS A MOST **LAMENTABLE** FAILING.

COME ALONG.

SO, YOU *HAD* TO PUT YOURSELF BEFORE HIS EYES, DID YOU? *HAD* TO CALL ATTENTION TO YOURSELF.

WELL, HE'S DECIDED WHAT TO DO WITH YOU.

I'M TO CHOOSE A HORSE FOR YOU TOMORROW. IT WILL BE AN OLDER, STEADIER BEAST THAT'S... LESS *IMPRESSIONABLE*.

SEE THAT YOU BEHAVE. I'LL *KNOW* IF YOU'RE PLAYING ABOUT.

YOU'LL BE UP WITH THE SUN FROM NOW ON, BOY. YOU'LL LEARN FROM ME IN THE MORNING.

CARING FOR A HORSE, AND MASTERING IT. HOW TO HUNT YOUR HOUNDS PROPERLY.

A *MAN'S* WAY OF CONTROLLING BEASTS IS WHAT I'LL TEACH YOU.

YES, SIR.

AFTERNOONS, *THEY'VE* GOT YOU, FOR WEAPONS AND SUCH. PROBABLY THE *SKILL*, EVENTUALLY.

IN WINTER MONTHS, THERE WILL BE INDOOR LEARNING. LANGUAGES AND SIGNS. WRITING AND READING AND NUMBERS. HISTORIES, TOO.

WHAT YOU'LL *DO* WITH IT ALL, I'VE NO IDEA, BUT MIND YOU LEARN IT WELL TO PLEASE THE KING.

HE'S *NOT* A MAN TO DISPLEASE, LET ALONE CROSS.

YOU'LL HAVE A PROPER ROOM OF YOUR OWN NOW, UP IN THE KEEP, WHERE ALL THOSE OF *NOBLE BLOOD* SLEEP.

YOU'D BE SLEEPING THERE RIGHT NOW, IF YOU'D BOTHERED TO COME IN ON TIME.

WHAT? I DON'T UNDERSTAND. A ROOM?

OH, SO YOU *CAN* BE SWIFT SPOKEN, WHEN YOU'VE A MIND?

YOU HEARD ME, BOY. YOU'LL HAVE A ROOM OF YOUR OWN, UP AT THE KEEP.

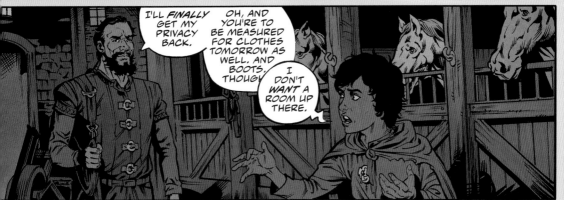

I'LL *FINALLY* GET MY PRIVACY BACK.

OH, AND YOU'RE TO BE MEASURED FOR CLOTHES TOMORROW AS WELL, AND BOOTS, THOUGH--

I DON'T *WANT* A ROOM UP THERE.

WELL, YOU'RE TO HAVE ONE, AND IT'S TIME AND PAST TIME FOR IT. YOU'RE *CHIVALRY'S* GET.

TO PUT YOU DOWN HERE IN THE STABLE, LIKE A STRAY PUP, WELL...

...IT'S JUST NOT *FITTING.*

I'D RATHER I *WAS* A STRAY PUP.

YOU WOULDN'T LET THEM DO THIS TO A STRAY PUP. CHANGING *EVERYTHING* ALL *AT ONCE.*

WHEN THEY GAVE THE BLOOD-HOUND PUPPY TO LORD GRIMSBY, YOU SENT YOUR OLD SHIRT WITH IT.

SO IT WOULD HAVE SOMETHING THAT SMELLED OF HOME UNTIL IT SETTLED IN.

WELL, I *DIDN'T...*

COME HERE, FITZ, COME HERE, BOY.

THERE'S NOTHING TO BE AFRAID OF.

AND, ANYWAY, THEY'VE ONLY TOLD US THAT YOU'RE TO *HAVE* A ROOM UP AT THE KEEP.

NO ONE'S SAID THAT YOU'VE GOT TO SLEEP IN IT *EVERY* NIGHT.

SOME NIGHTS, IF THINGS ARE A BIT TOO QUIET FOR YOU, YOU CAN FIND YOUR WAY DOWN HERE.

DOES THAT SOUND *RIGHT* TO YOU?

...I *SUPPOSE* SO.

YOU DON'T THINK SHE'S MUCH, DO YOU?

WELL, HOW MUCH OF A HORSE DID YOU HAVE *YESTERDAY,* FITZ?

MEASUREMENTS AND COLORING ARE MUCH THE SAME AS CHIVALRY'S WERE AT HIS AGE.

QUITE A *MERCY* THAT PATIENCE NEVER HAS TO SEE THE BOY.

CHIVALRY'S STAMP IS MUCH TOO PLAIN ON HIS FACE TO LEAVE HER ANY PRIDE AT ALL.

MASTER? HAVE YOU FINISHED EATING?

WHILE YOU'RE HEARING ALL THIS VITAL GOSSIP, I *MIGHT* POINT OUT TO YOU THAT NO WISE MAN TELLS ALL HE KNOWS.

AND THAT HE WHO CARRIES TALES HAS *LITTLE ELSE* IN HIS HEAD. DO YOU UNDERSTAND ME, BRANT?

...I THINK SO, MA'AM.

YOU THINK SO? THEN I SHALL BE *PLAINER.* STOP BEING A *NOSY LITTLE GOSSIP* AND ATTEND TO YOUR CHORES.

YOU, BOY. FOLLOW ME.

I'VE BEEN SENT FOR LESSONS... WITH HOD.

I'M TO BE TAUGHT... ARMS AND WEAPONRY.

MMM.

CHOOSE ONE.

HADN'T I BETTER WAIT FOR HOD?

I *AM* HOD. NOW PICK YOURSELF A STAVE, BOY. I WANT TO SEE WHAT YOU'RE *MADE* OF, AND WHAT YOU *KNOW.*

BOY, WHAT ARE YOU CALLED?

FITZ IS WHAT BURRICH CALLS ME.

HE *WOULD.* CALLS A BITCH A BITCH, AND A BASTARD A BASTARD.

I SUPPOSE I SEE HIS REASONS. FITZ YOU ARE, AND FITZ YOU'LL BE CALLED BY *ME* AS WELL.

NOW. I SHALL SHOW YOU WHY THE POLE YOU SELECTED WAS TOO LONG FOR YOU, AND TOO THICK.

AND *THEN* YOU SHALL SELECT ANOTHER.

My life went 'round in its new settled routine.

But despite my schedule, I found myself mostly alone.

Loneliness.

It found me every night as I vainly tried to find a small and cozy spot in my big bed.

When I had slept above the stables, the dreams of the well-used animals below had been heathery.

Like the sweet rising waft from a baking of good bread.

But now, isolated in a room walled with stone...

...I finally had time for all those devouring, aching dreams that are the portion of humans.

How my father and my mother both could have dismissed me from their lives so easily.

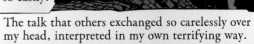

The talk that others exchanged so carelessly over my head, interpreted in my own terrifying way.

But mostly I ached with loneliness, for in all that great keep, there were none I sensed as friend.

None save the beasts, and Burrich had forbidden me to have any closeness with them.

Chapter Four

HURRY UP, BOY.

IT IS A MESS. *MORE* THAN A MESS, I SUPPOSE. BUT, WELL...

...IT'S BEEN A WHILE, I SUPPOSE. AND *LONGER* THAN A WHILE.

IT IS A BIT NIPPY TO BE STANDING ABOUT IN JUST A NIGHTSHIRT.

THIS WAY, BOY.

INTRODUCTIONS ARE IN ORDER.

FIRST, LET ME INTRODUCE YOU TO *YOURSELF.*

YOUR PEDIGREE IS WRITTEN *ALL OVER* YOU.

SHREWD CHOSE TO ACKNOWLEDGE IT, FOR ALL HIS DENIALS WOULDN'T HAVE SUFFICED TO CONVINCE *ANYONE* OTHERWISE.

"BURRICH'S SHOWN YOU BOTH HOW TO *WORK* AND HOW TO *OBEY.* TWO THINGS THAT BURRICH HIMSELF EXCELS AT.

"YOU'RE NOT ESPECIALLY STRONG, OR FAST, OR BRIGHT. *DON'T* THINK YOU ARE.

"BUT YOU'LL HAVE THE *STUBBORNNESS* TO WEAR DOWN ANYONE STRONGER, OR FASTER, OR BRIGHTER THAN YOURSELF.

"AND THAT'S MORE OF A DANGER TO *YOU* THAN TO ANYONE ELSE."

BUT THAT IS *NOT* WHAT IS NOW MOST IMPORTANT ABOUT YOU.

"YOU ARE THE *KING'S MAN* NOW.

"HE FEEDS YOU. HE CLOTHES YOU. HE SEES YOU ARE EDUCATED."

AND ALL HE ASKS IN RETURN, FOR NOW, IS YOUR *LOYALTY.*

LATER, HE WILL ASK YOUR *SERVICE.*

THOSE ARE THE CONDITIONS UNDER WHICH I WILL TEACH YOU. THAT YOU ARE THE KING'S MAN, AND LOYAL TO HIM *COMPLETELY.*

FOR IF YOU ARE *OTHERWISE,* IT WOULD BE TOO DANGEROUS TO EDUCATE YOU IN MY ART.

DO YOU AGREE?

I DO.

I GIVE YOU MY WORD.

GOOD. NOW, ON TO OTHER THINGS.

DO YOU KNOW WHO I AM, BOY? OR WHY YOU'RE HERE?

NO.

WELL, NO ONE ELSE DOES EITHER. SO YOU MIND IT STAYS THAT WAY.

SPEAK TO NO ONE OF WHAT WE DO HERE, NOR OF ANYTHING YOU LEARN. UNDER-STAND THAT?

YES.

GOOD. NOW, YOU CAN CALL ME CHADE. AND I SHALL CALL YOU BOY.

THAT'S NOT NAMES FOR EITHER OF US, BUT THEY'LL DO, FOR THE TIME WE'LL HAVE TOGETHER.

SO, I'M CHADE, AND I'M YET ANOTHER TEACHER THAT SHREWD HAS FOUND FOR YOU.

IT TOOK HIM A WHILE TO REMEMBER I WAS HERE, AND THEN IT TOOK HIM A SPACE TO NERVE HIMSELF TO ASK ME.

AS TO WHAT I'M TO TEACH YOU... WELL...

...IT'S MURDER, MORE OR LESS.

KILLING PEOPLE.

THE *FINE ART* OF DIPLOMATIC *ASSASSINATION.*

OR BLINDING, OR DEAFENING. OR A WEAKENING OF THE LIMBS, OR A PARALYSIS OR A DEBILITATING COUGH.

OR IMPOTENCY. OR EARLY SENILITY, OR INSANITY. *OR...* BUT IT DOESN'T MATTER.

IT'S *ALL* BEEN MY TRADE.

AND IT WILL BE YOURS.

IF YOU AGREE.

I'M GOING TO BE TEACHING YOU HOW TO KILL PEOPLE FOR YOUR KING.

THE *NASTY, FURTIVE, POLITE* WAYS TO KILL PEOPLE.

YOU'LL EITHER DEVELOP A *TASTE* FOR IT, OR NOT. BUT I'LL MAKE SURE YOU KNOW *HOW.*

AND I'LL MAKE SURE OF ONE *OTHER* THING, FOR THAT WAS THE STIPULATION I MADE WITH KING SHREWD.

"THAT YOU *KNOW* WHAT YOU ARE LEARNING, AS I NEVER DID WHEN I WAS YOUR AGE."

SO. I'M TO TEACH YOU TO BE AN ASSASSIN.

IS THAT ALL RIGHT WITH YOU, BOY?

BOY, I CAN TEACH YOU EVEN IF YOU HATE ME. I CAN TEACH YOU IF YOU ARE BORED, OR LAZY OR STUPID.

BUT I CAN'T TEACH YOU IF YOU'RE *AFRAID* TO SPEAK TO ME. AT LEAST, NOT THE WAY I *WANT* TO TEACH YOU.

AND I CAN'T TEACH YOU IF YOU DECIDE THIS IS SOMETHING YOU'D RATHER NOT LEARN.

BUT YOU HAVE TO *TELL* ME.

YOU'VE LEARNED TO GUARD YOUR THOUGHTS *SO* WELL, YOU'RE ALMOST AFRAID TO LET *YOURSELF* KNOW WHAT THEY ARE.

BUT TRY SPEAKING THEM ALOUD NOW, TO ME. YOU *WON'T* BE PUNISHED.

I DON'T MUCH LIKE IT.

THE IDEA OF *KILLING* PEOPLE.

AH.

NEITHER DID *I*, WHEN IT CAME DOWN TO IT. NOR DO I, STILL.

AS EACH TIME COMES, YOU'LL *DECIDE*. THE FIRST TIME WILL BE HARDEST.

BUT KNOW THAT THAT DECISION IS *MANY* YEARS AWAY. AND IN THE MEANTIME, YOU HAVE *MUCH* TO LEARN.

YOU SHOULD REMEMBER THIS IN EVERY SITUATION NOT JUST THIS ONE: LEARNING IS *NEVER* WRONG.

EVEN LEARNING HOW TO KILL ISN'T *WRONG*. OR *RIGHT*. IT'S JUST A THING I CAN TEACH YOU. THAT'S ALL.

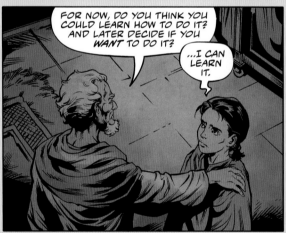

FOR NOW, DO YOU THINK YOU COULD LEARN HOW TO DO IT? AND LATER DECIDE IF YOU *WANT* TO DO IT?

...I CAN LEARN IT.

GOOD. THAT'S WELL ENOUGH, THEN. WELL ENOUGH.

WE MAY AS WELL BEGIN TONIGHT.

LET'S START BY *TIDYING UP*. THERE'S A BROOM OVER THERE.

SEEMS *FAMILIAR,* DOESN'T IT, BOY?

MY FACE, I MEAN.

DON'T TROUBLE YOURSELF ABOUT IT, BOY.

IT LEAVES ITS TRACKS ON *ALL* OF US.

"SOONER OR LATER, YOU'LL GET THE TUMBLE OF IT.

"NOW, YOU'LL REMEMBER THAT THIS IS ALL A VERY DARK SECRET, WON'T YOU?

"NOT JUST ME AND THIS ROOM, BUT THE *WHOLE THING.*

"WAKING UP AT NIGHT AND LESSONS IN HOW TO KILL PEOPLE, AND ALL OF IT."

MASTER? YOU SHOULD *ALREADY* BE AWAKE.

YOU'RE *LATE* FOR YOUR LESSONS.

I'LL LEAVE YOU TO GET READY.

TARDINESS? I EXPECT *BETTER* OF YOU, FITZ.

BASTARD YOU MAY BE, BUT YOU'RE *CHIVALRY'S BASTARD*, AND I'LL MAKE YOU A MAN HE'LL BE PROUD OF.

DON'T THINK THAT BECAUSE YOU'VE A *ROOM* UP IN THE CASTLE AND A *CREST* ON YOUR JERKIN...

...THAT YOU CAN TURN INTO SOME *SPRAWL-ABOUT ROGUE* WHO SNORES IN HIS BED UNTIL ALL HOURS. I'LL *NOT* HAVE IT.

YOU MEAN HOW *REGAL* IS, DON'T YOU?

NEITHER YOU NOR I ARE IN A POSITION TO CRITICIZE *ANY* OF THE PRINCES.

I MEANT ONLY AS A *GENERAL RULE* THAT SLEEPING THE MORNING AWAY ILL BEFITS A MAN. AND EVEN *LESS* SO A BOY.

AND *NEVER* A PRINCE.

YOUR FATHER *NEVER* SLEPT PAST THE SUN'S MIDPOINT BECAUSE HE'D BEEN DRINKING THE NIGHT BEFORE.

OF COURSE, HE HAD A HEAD FOR WINE LIKE I'VE *NEVER* SEEN SINCE. BUT THERE WAS *DISCIPLINE* TO IT, TOO.

"HE EXPECTED THOSE IN HIS COMMAND TO *FOLLOW* HIS EXAMPLE. IT DIDN'T ALWAYS MAKE HIM POPULAR, BUT HIS SOLDIERS *RESPECTED* HIM.

"THAT WAS HOW CHIVALRY RULED. BY *EXAMPLE*, AND BY THE *GRACE* OF HIS WORDS. SO SHOULD ANY *REAL* PRINCE DO."

I'M NOT A *REAL* PRINCE. I'M A *BASTARD*.

BE YOUR *BLOOD*, BOY, AND IGNORE WHAT ANYONE ELSE THINKS OF YOU.

SOMETIMES I GET *TIRED* OF DOING THE HARD THINGS.

SO DO I.

I *DON'T* ASK ANY MORE OF YOU THAN I ASK OF *MYSELF*.

...I KNOW THAT.

I JUST WANT TO DO MY *BEST* BY YOU.

BECAUSE IF YOU COULD MAKE CHIVALRY *PROUD* OF ME, OF WHAT YOU'D MADE ME *INTO*...

...THEN MAYBE HE WOULD COME *BACK?*

NO. I *DON'T* THINK THAT.

"I DON'T SUPPOSE *ANYTHING* WOULD MAKE HIM COME BACK.

"AND EVEN IF HE *DID*, HE WOULDN'T BE WHO HE WAS. *BEFORE*, I MEAN."

IT'S ALL *MY* FAULT HE WENT AWAY, ISN'T IT?

I DON'T SUPPOSE IT'S *ANY* MAN'S FAULT THAT HE'S BORN. AND THERE'S CERTAINLY *NO* WAY A BABE CAN MAKE ITSELF NOT A BASTARD.

NO. CHIVALRY BROUGHT HIS DOWNFALL ON *HIMSELF*, THOUGH THAT'S A HARD THING FOR ME TO SAY.

AND *YOUR* DOWN-FALL, TOO.

I DO WELL ENOUGH FOR MYSELF, FITZ. I DO WELL ENOUGH.

YOUR TONGUE'S WAGGING LIKE THE *TOWN GOSSIP* TODAY, FITZ. WHAT'S GOT *INTO* YOU?

...THEY'RE JUST THINGS I'VE *WONDERED* ABOUT FOR A LONG TIME.

But it was really about Chade. About someone who wanted me to understand and have a say in what I was learning.

It had freed up my tongue to finally ask all the questions I'd been carrying about for years.

WELL, IT'S AN *IMPROVEMENT* THAT YOU ASK, THOUGH I WON'T ALWAYS PROMISE YOU AN ANSWER.

AND IT'S GOOD TO HEAR YOU SPEAK LIKE A *MAN*. MAKES ME WORRY LESS ABOUT LOSING YOU TO THE *BEASTS*.

I grew to look forward to my dark-time encounters with Chade.

They never had a schedule, nor any pattern that I could discern.

A week, even two, might go by between meetings.

Or he might summon me every night for a week, leaving me staggering about my daytime chores.

It was a strenuous schedule for a growing boy, yet I never thought of complaining or refusing one of Chade's calls.

Nor do I think it ever occurred to him that my night lessons presented a difficulty for me.

Nocturnal himself, it must have seemed a perfectly natural time for him to be teaching me.

And the lessons I learned were oddly suited to the darker hours of the world.

There were many games we played. These were the lessons in my assassin's primer.

One evening might be spent in my laborious study of herbals…

…with the requirement that the next day I was to collect six samples that matched those illustrations.

I found myself meeting and coming to know a good many of the lesser folk.

Then I'd that evening report the entire conversation back to Chade, as close to word perfect as I could.

Soon he began to use me for small jobs about the keep.

Tricks that convinced a visiting noble to extend their stay.

There was one task that absolutely delighted me, an assignment that I knew was more than a whim of Chade's.

A number of nobles had gathered at Buckkeep to form a council to discuss the increase in Outislander raids.

This included Lord Jessup and his Lady. Although Lady Dahlia spent most of her time exploring Buckkeep.

Chade told me the Lady's page would deliver something to Regal's room. I was to remove the object.

From the way the girl slipped in, I was convinced this was not her first mission.

Chade would give me a question to approach them with, interests to feign.

Later I realized that the memory exercise was also instruction in how to befriend the commoner folk.

And I learned to lie very well. I do not think it was taught me accidentally.

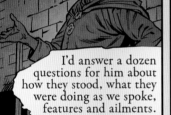

I'd answer a dozen questions for him about how they stood, what they were doing as we spoke, features and ailments.

Chade taught me sleight of hand and the art of moving stealthily. Where to strike a man to render him unconscious.

Where to stab a man so that he dies without too much blood welling out.

I think the most difficult part of the task was refraining from opening the scroll I recovered for Chade.

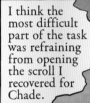

Over the next few days I waited, certain there would be some sort of furor.

However, Regal remained his usual self, save that he was even sharper than usual.

Lady Dahlia suddenly took an interest in the council proceedings, becoming an ardent supporter of warship taxes.

The whole thing mystified me, but when I at last mentioned it to Chade, he rebuked me.

"Only Shrewd may plan the moves and plot his game," Chade reminded me.

"You and I, we are playing pieces. But we are the **best** of his markers. Be assured of that."

But early on, Chade found the limits of my obedience.

Come late fall of that year, on the very cusp of winter's tooth, I was given my most difficult assignment.

...THEY THOUGHT IT A PRANK BY WATER SPRITES, THAT *EVERY* SHIRT IN THE LAUNDRY COURTYARD WAS TURNED INSIDE OUT.

YOU'VE A *GIFT* FOR THIS, BOY. I *ALMOST* THINK THERE'S NO TASK I COULD SET YOU THAT YOU COULDN'T DO.

BUT I'VE A *CHALLENGE* FOR YOU. IT *WON'T* BE EASY, EVEN FOR ONE WITH AS LIGHT A TOUCH AS YOURS.

TRY ME.

...PERHAPS WE'D BEST *WAIT* ANOTHER MONTH OR TWO, WHEN YOU'VE HAD A BIT MORE TEACHING.

I'VE A GAME TO TEACH YOU TONIGHT, ONE THAT WILL SHARPEN YOUR EYE AND YOUR MEMORY.

WERE THERE ANY YELLOW ONES?

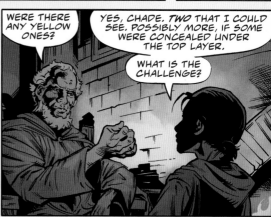

YES, CHADE. *TWO* THAT I COULD SEE. POSSIBLY MORE, IF SOME WERE CONCEALED UNDER THE TOP LAYER.

WHAT IS THE CHALLENGE?

RIGHT YOU WERE. ONLY TWO YELLOW ONES. SHALL WE GO *AGAIN?*

CHADE, I *CAN* DO IT.

YOU *THINK* SO, DO YOU?

LOOK AGAIN, HERE'S THE STONES.

WERE THERE ANY *RED* ONES?

YES.

CHADE, *WHAT* IS THE TASK?

TO BRING ME SOMETHING PERSONAL FROM THE *KING'S* NIGHT TABLE.

NOW, WERE THERE MORE RED ONES THAN BLUE?

WHAT?

WRONG, BOY! THREE RED AND THREE BLUE. EXACTLY THE SAME.

AND SEVEN GREEN. I *KNEW* THAT, CHADE. BUT...

...YOU WANT ME TO *STEAL* FROM THE *KING?*

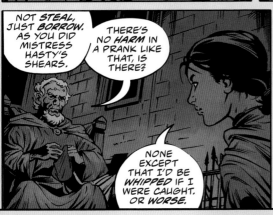

NOT *STEAL,* JUST *BORROW.* AS YOU DID MISTRESS HASTY'S SHEARS.

THERE'S NO *HARM* IN A PRANK LIKE THAT, IS THERE?

NONE EXCEPT THAT I'D BE *WHIPPED* IF I WERE CAUGHT. OR *WORSE.*

AND YOU'RE *AFRAID* YOU'D BE CAUGHT.

SEE, I *TOLD* YOU IT HAD BEST WAIT A MONTH OR TWO, UNTIL YOUR SKILLS WERE *BETTER.*

IT'S *NOT* THE PUNISHMENT. IT'S THAT IF I WERE CAUGHT...

"THE KING AND I... WE MADE A *BARGAIN.*"

YOUR STUDIES PROCEED WELL, BY ALL ACCOUNTING.

AND DO YOU FEEL I AM KEEPING MY BARGAIN WITH YOU?

SIR, I *DO.*

THEN SEE THAT YOU KEEP *YOUR* END OF IT AS WELL.

IT'S JUST A BIT OF *MISCHIEF*, BOY. THAT'S *ALL*. IT'S NOT REALLY SO SERIOUS AS YOU SEEM TO *THINK* IT.

THE *ONLY* REASON I'M CHOOSING IT AS A TASK IS THAT THE KING'S ROOM AND HIS THINGS ARE SO CLOSELY WATCHED.

WE'RE TALKING ABOUT A *REAL* BIT OF STEALTH NOW, TO ENTER THE KING'S OWN CHAMBERS AND TAKE SOMETHING OF HIS.

IF YOU COULD DO *THAT*, I'D BELIEVE I'D SPENT MY TIME *WELL* HERE. I'D FEEL YOU *APPRECIATED* WHAT I'D TAUGHT YOU.

YOU *KNOW* I APPRECIATE WHAT YOU TEACH ME.

I'D FEEL... *DISLOYAL*. LIKE I WAS USING WHAT YOU'D TAUGHT ME TO *TRICK* THE KING.

ALMOST AS IF I WERE *LAUGHING* AT HIM.

AH! DON'T LET THAT BOTHER YOU. KING SHREWD CAN APPRECIATE A GOOD JEST WHEN HE'S SHOWN ONE.

WHATEVER YOU TAKE, I'LL RETURN IT MYSELF. IT WILL BE A *SIGN* TO HIM OF HOW WELL I'VE TAUGHT YOU.

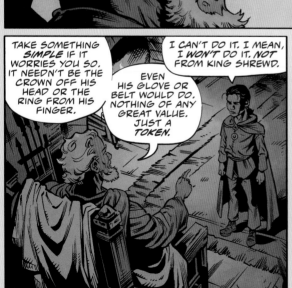

TAKE SOMETHING *SIMPLE* IF IT WORRIES YOU SO. IT NEEDN'T BE THE CROWN OFF HIS HEAD OR THE RING FROM HIS FINGER.

EVEN HIS GLOVE OR BELT WOULD DO. NOTHING OF ANY GREAT VALUE. JUST A *TOKEN*.

I CAN'T DO IT. I MEAN, I *WON'T* DO IT. *NOT* FROM KING SHREWD.

I PROMISED TO BE *LOYAL* TO SHREWD. AND THIS--

THERE'S NOTHING *DISLOYAL* ABOUT THIS!

WHAT ARE YOU *SAYING*, BOY? THAT I'M ASKING YOU TO *BETRAY* YOUR KING? DON'T BE AN *IDIOT*.

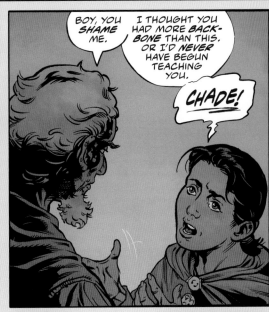

Chapter Five

Even now, I do not like to recall the days after Chade dismissed me so coldly.

I hunched through them, so sick at heart that I could not properly eat or rest.

I could not focus my mind on any task.

I took the rebukes that my teachers gave me with bleak acceptance.

The very thought of eating made me weary.

The depth of bleakness that settled over me was too solid for me to fight.

All of my possible choices led to gray ends, until I could not face the futility of getting out of bed.

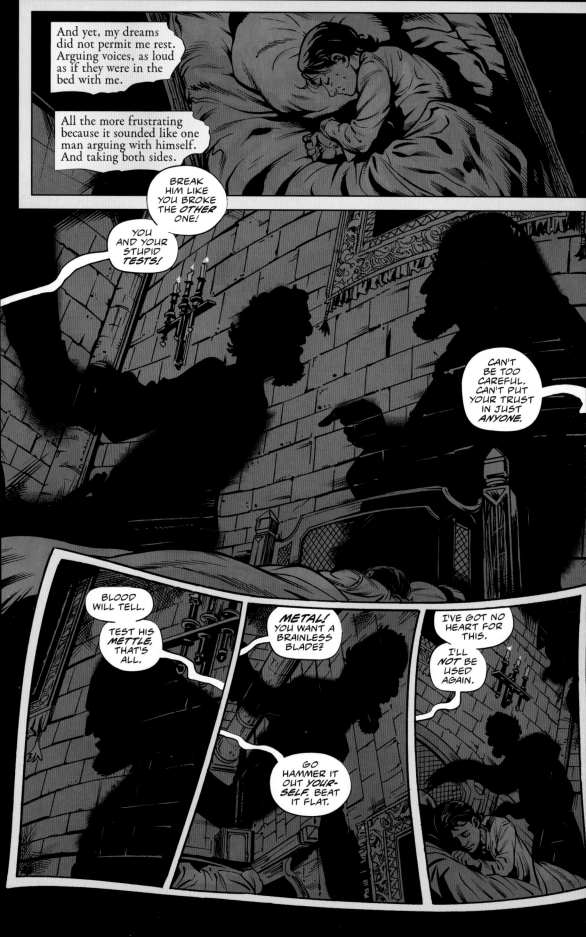

hot stay

THERE. THAT SIDE'S COOLER.

THERE'S *NOTHING* THE MATTER WITH YOU THAT I'VE EVER SEEN BEFORE, FITZ.

AT LEAST, WHATEVER'S AILING YOU ISN'T IN YOUR GUTS OR YOUR BLOOD.

IF YOU WERE A BIT OLDER, I'D SUSPECT YOU HAD *WOMAN* PROBLEMS.

YOU ACT LIKE A SOLDIER ON A THREE-DAY DRUNK, BUT WITHOUT THE WINE.

BOY, WHAT'S THE **MATTER** WITH YOU?

here together

I'M JUST SO ALONE NOW.

ALONE? FITZ, I'M **RIGHT HERE.**

HOW CAN YOU SAY YOU'RE ALONE?

I'LL FIX YOU A PLATE.

I'M NOT--

HUH.

COME HERE, FITZ.

THERE ISN'T MUCH IN A MAN'S HEAD THAT CAN'T BE CURED BY WORKING...

...AND TAKING CARE OF *SOMETHING* ELSE.

THE RAT DOG WHELPED A FEW DAYS AGO, AND THIS PUP IS TOO *WEAK* TO COMPETE WITH THE OTHERS.

SEE IF YOU CAN KEEP HIM *ALIVE* TODAY.

ENOUGH OF THAT.

THAT'S NOT A THING FOR A MAN TO DO.

AAAH

AND IT WON'T SOLVE WHATEVER IS CHEWING ON YOUR SOUL.

GIVE THE PUP BACK TO HIS MOTHER.

C'MON. BETTING ALL THAT WORK FINALLY WOKE UP YOUR BELLY.

I KNOW YOU'VE HAD ALE AND WINE BEFORE...

...BUT IT SEEMS TIME YOU LEARN HOW *GROWN MEN* DRINK.

ARE YOU *MAD?* GIVING STRONG SPIRITS LIKE THAT TO A *MERE BOY?*

TRICK IS TO GET IT ALL DOWN BEFORE THE BURN *REALLY* TAKES HOLD...

EASY, FITZ.

NOW YOU'LL SLEEP.

AND TOMORROW WE'LL DO THE SAME *AGAIN*.

AND. *AGAIN*.

UNTIL ONE DAY YOU GET UP AND FIND OUT THAT WHATEVER IT WAS *DIDN'T* KILL YOU AFTER ALL.

But I still didn't sleep.

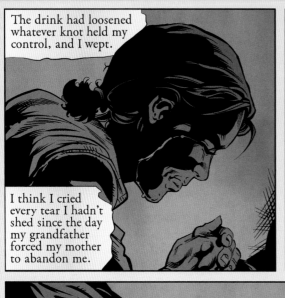

The drink had loosened whatever knot held my control, and I wept.

I think I cried every tear I hadn't shed since the day my grandfather forced my mother to abandon me.

MERE!

YOU WERE RIGHT.

YOU WERE RIGHT.

I WAS ASKING YOU TO DO SOMETHING WRONG.

AND YOU WERE *RIGHT* TO REFUSE IT.

YOU *WON'T* BE TESTED THAT WAY AGAIN.

NOT BY ME.

"UGGHH..."

EDA'S MERCY...

♪♪♫

HAS HIS FATHER'S HEAD FOR SPIRITS...

I'LL HANDLE THE CHORES TODAY.

YOU TAKE THAT WHISTLING SOMEWHERE ELSE.

KNEW THAT WOULD DO YOU SOME GOOD...

Three days later King Shrewd summoned me in the dawn.

COME. SIT.

The King serving me food with his own hand...

...the gesture was not lost on me.

IT WAS *MY* IDEA. NOT *HIS*.

HE *NEVER* APPROVED OF IT. I *INSISTED*.

WHEN YOU'RE OLDER, YOU'LL UNDERSTAND. I CAN TAKE NO CHANCES, NOT ON *ANYONE.*

BUT I PROMISED HIM THAT YOU'D KNOW THIS RIGHT FROM *ME.*

IT WAS ALL MY OWN IDEA, NEVER HIS. AND I WILL *NEVER* ASK HIM TO TRY YOUR METTLE IN SUCH A WAY AGAIN.

ON THAT, YOU HAVE A *KING'S WORD.*

It was as if there had never been a pause in our lessons.

...BE PREPARED TO REPORT ON THE CONVERSATION TOMORROW NIGHT, BOY.

YES, CHADE.

NOW, I BELIEVE WE'RE--

KRAK

We never spoke of that moment.

But I believe that the knife is still there.

Chapter Six

There are two traditions about the custom of giving royal offspring names suggestive of virtues or abilities.

The one most commonly held is that these names are binding, that the Skill melds the name to the child.

The child cannot help but grow up to practice the virtue ascribed to him or her by name.

A more ancient tradition attributes such names to accident, at least initially.

It is said that King Taker and King Ruler, the first two Outislanders to rule, had no such names at all.

Rather, their names in their own tongue were very similar in sound to those words in the Duchies' tongue.

They thus came to be known by their homonyms rather than by their true names.

YOU'VE FORGOTTEN TO CROSS THEIR TAILS. OTHER THAN THAT, YOUR LETTERING IS *MUCH* IMPROVED.

But for the purposes of royalty...

...it is better the common folk believe a child given a noble name must grow to have a noble nature.

NOT ONLY ON THESE *DUCHIAN* CHARACTERS, BUT ON THE *OUT-ISLANDER* RUNES AS WELL.

I DON'T KNOW WHO TO ASK THIS OF, EXCEPT *YOU*. PROPERLY, I'D ASK YOUR PARENTS, BUT...

...WINTER'S SOON OVER, AND I'LL BE WANDERING THE SIX DUCHIES, GETTING HERBS AND BERRIES AND ROOTS FOR MY INKS AND PAPERS.

IT'S A GOOD LIFE, *SCRIBING*. WALKING FREE ON THE ROADS IN SUMMERS AND GUESTING AT THE KEEP ALL WINTER.

I TAKE AN APPRENTICE, EVERY FEW YEARS. WHAT WOULD *YOU* THINK ABOUT BECOMING A SCRIBE?

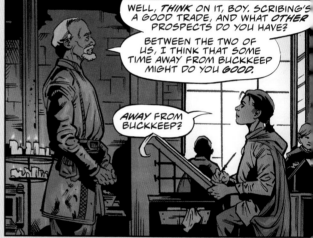

WELL, *THINK* ON IT, BOY. SCRIBING'S A GOOD TRADE, AND WHAT *OTHER* PROSPECTS DO YOU HAVE?

BETWEEN THE TWO OF US, I THINK THAT SOME TIME AWAY FROM BUCKKEEP MIGHT DO YOU *GOOD*.

AWAY FROM BUCKKEEP?

YES. AS YOU GROW OLDER CHIVALRY'S SHADOW WILL GROW *THINNER*. IT WILL NOT ALWAYS SHELTER YOU.

BETTER YOU WERE YOUR *OWN* MAN, WITH YOUR *OWN* LIFE, BEFORE HIS PROTECTION IS ENTIRELY GONE.

YOU DON'T HAVE TO ANSWER ME NOW. *THINK* ABOUT IT.

DISCUSS IT WITH BURRICH, PERHAPS.

"*NO*. NO MATTER WHERE YOU WENT, YOU WOULD STILL BE CHIVALRY'S BASTARD."

FEDWREN IS MORE *PERSPICACIOUS* THAN I BELIEVED HIM TO BE, BUT HE STILL DOESN'T UNDERSTAND. NOT THE *WHOLE* PICTURE.

AWAY FROM HERE, YOU WOULD BECOME A *THREAT* TO KING SHREWD, AND A *GREATER* THREAT TO HIS HEIRS AFTER HIM.

"YOU WOULD HAVE NO SIMPLE LIFE OF FREEDOM AS A WANDERING SCRIBE.

"RATHER YOU WOULD BE FOUND IN YOUR INN BED WITH YOUR *THROAT CUT*, OR WITH AN *ARROW* THROUGH YOU ON THE HIGH ROAD."

BUT *WHY?*

BECAUSE YOU'RE A *ROYAL BASTARD*, HOSTAGE TO YOUR OWN BLOODLINES. AND THESE ARE *RESTLESS TIMES*.

"THE OUTISLANDERS GROW *BRAVER* ABOUT THEIR RAIDS. THE COAST FOLK WANT *MORE* PATROL SHIPS, EVEN WARSHIPS OF THEIR OWN.

"THE INLAND DUCHIES WANT *NO* PART OF PAYING FOR SHIPS, ESPECIALLY IF IT MIGHT PRECIPITATE US INTO A FULL-SCALE WAR.

"THE MOUNTAIN FOLK ARE BECOMING *MORE CHARY* ABOUT THE USE OF THEIR PASSES. THE TRADE FEES GROW *STEEPER* EVERY MONTH.

"TO THE SOUTH, IN SANDSEDGE AND BEYOND, THERE IS *DROUGHT*, AND TIMES ARE *HARD*.

"VERITY IS NEITHER THE SOLDIER NOR THE DIPLOMAT THAT *CHIVALRY* WAS. IF THINGS DO NOT IMPROVE, PEOPLE WILL TALK.

"'A BASTARD'S NOT *SO* LARGE A THING TO MAKE A FUSS OVER,' THEY'LL SAY. 'WERE *CHIVALRY* IN POWER, HE'D PUT A STOP TO ALL THIS.'"

SO CHIVALRY MIGHT YET BECOME KING?

NO, BOY. EVEN IF THE FOLK ALL WANTED HIM TO, I DOUBT HE'D GO AGAINST THE KING'S WISHES.

BUT IT WOULD CAUSE MUMBLINGS AND GRUMBLINGS, RIOTS AND SKIRMISHES, A *BAD* CLIMATE FOR A BASTARD.

I'M NEVER GOING TO GET TO GO *ANYWHERE,* AM I?

YOU'LL GET TO GO *MANY* PLACES.

QUIETLY, AND WHEN THE FAMILY INTERESTS *REQUIRE* YOU TO GO THERE.

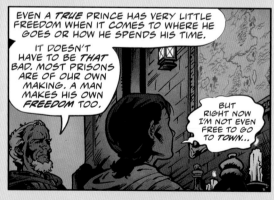

EVEN A *TRUE* PRINCE HAS VERY LITTLE FREEDOM WHEN IT COMES TO WHERE HE GOES OR HOW HE SPENDS HIS TIME.

IT DOESN'T HAVE TO BE *THAT* BAD. MOST PRISONS ARE OF OUR OWN MAKING. A MAN MAKES HIS OWN *FREEDOM* TOO.

BUT RIGHT NOW I'M NOT EVEN FREE TO GO TO *TOWN...*

AND IT'S THAT *IMPORTANT* TO YOU? TO GO DOWN TO A GRUBBY, GREASY LITTLE PORT LIKE BUCKKEEP TOWN?

THERE ARE *OTHER* PEOPLE THERE...

...THEY CALL ME *NEWBOY.* AND THEY DON'T THINK *"THE BASTARD"* EVERY TIME THEY LOOK AT ME.

MMM.

NOW, REGARDING *UNDETECTABLE POISONS...*

It was two days later that Fedwren gave me a list of supplies he required from town, and enough silver to buy them.

I went out of the gates with two extra coppers for myself and my brain giddy with sudden freedom.

I counted up the months since I had last slipped away, and was shocked to find it had been a year or better.

I planned to renew my old familiarity with the town. No one had told me when I had to return.

The variety of items on Fedwren's list took me all over, from the merchant shops to the harbor bazaar.

KEPPET.

It was at the latter that, quite unexpectedly, a familiar face met my eyes.

A year had passed since I'd last seen her.

How could a person change so much?

...BEEN WEARING SKIRTS FOR SEVERAL MONTHS NOW. *QUITE* PREFER THEM TO TROUSERS.

THESE WERE MY MOTHER'S. ONE SIMPLY *CAN'T* GET WOOL WOVEN THIS FINE ANYMORE, OR A RED DYED AS BRIGHT.

WHAT BRINGS *YOU* TO TOWN IN SUCH FINE GARMENTS?

OH, I...

...I'M ON ERRANDS FOR THE WRITING MASTER AT THE KEEP.

HE *IS* IN NEED OF TWO BEESWAX TAPERS.

I CAN *CERTAINLY* HELP WITH THOSE.

I MAKE THE BEST SCENTED CANDLES IN BUCKKEEP NOW, *EVERYONE* SAYS SO. IT'S THE BEESWAX.

BEESWAX TAKES THE SCENT *MUCH* BETTER THAN TALLOW, IN MY OPINION. I'VE BEEN TRYING TO RE-CREATE SOME OF MY MA'S RECIPES...

I *KNOW* THE THRESHER'S ROOT. SOME USE IT TO MAKE AN OINTMENT FOR SORE SHOULDERS AND BACKS.

BUT IF YOU DISTILL A TINCTURE FROM IT AND MIX IT WELL IN WINE, IT'S *NEVER* TASTED.

IT WILL MAKE A GROWN MAN SLEEP A DAY AND A NIGHT AND A DAY AGAIN, OR MAKE A CHILD DIE IN HIS SLEEP.

HOW... ...HOW DO YOU KNOW SUCH THINGS?!

I...I HEARD AN OLD TRAVELING MIDWIFE TALKING TO OUR MIDWIFE UP TO THE KEEP.

IT WAS... A *SAD* STORY SHE TOLD, OF AN INJURED MAN GIVEN SOME TO HELP HIM REST, BUT HIS BABY GOT INTO IT AS WELL.

A VERY, VERY SAD STORY.

I ONLY TELL IT TO BE SURE YOU ARE *CAREFUL* OF THE ROOT. DON'T LEAVE IT ABOUT WHERE ANY CHILD CAN GET AT IT.

THANK YOU. I *SHAN'T*.

ARE YOU INTERESTED IN HERBS AND ROOTS? I DIDN'T KNOW A SCRIBE *CARED* ABOUT SUCH THINGS.

OH, FEDWREN USES MANY THINGS, FOR HIS DYES AND INKS. SOME COPIES HE MAKES QUITE PLAIN, BUT OTHERS ARE FANCY.

HE SHOWED ME AN HERBAL WITH THE GREENS AND FLOWERS OF EACH HERB DONE AS THE BORDER FOR THE PAGE.

THAT I SHOULD DEARLY *LOVE* TO SEE.

I *MIGHT* BE ABLE TO GET YOU A COPY TO READ.

NOT TO *KEEP*, BUT TO STUDY FOR A FEW DAYS.

AS IF *I* COULD READ!

OH, BUT I IMAGINE YOU'VE PICKED UP SOME LETTERS, RUNNING ABOUT FOR THE SCRIBE'S ERRANDS.

MORE THAN JUST *SOME* LETTERS.

I CAN READ THIS *WHOLE THING.* ALL SEVEN ITEMS.

DO YOU THINK YOU COULD READ SOMETHING FOR ME?

OR EVEN ANY *PART* OF IT?

I'LL TRY.

MY FATHER'S IN THE SHOP. BE NOT *TOO* FAMILIAR WITH ME.

I'M TO GET SCRIBE FEDWREN TWO BEESWAX TAPERS. I DARE *NOT* GO BACK TO THE KEEP WITHOUT THEM.

Chade had taught me well. I looked to the man's fingernails and lips.

Even from across the room, I knew he could not live much longer.

Perhaps he no longer beat Molly because he no longer had the strength.

NOW THAT I WEAR SKIRTS, MY FATHER HAS GIVEN ME MY MOTHER'S THINGS.

I HAVE SOME TABLETS SHE WROTE. I'D LIKE TO KNOW WHAT THEY *SAY.*

Four were carefully precise accounts of herbal recipes for healing candles.

As I read each one softly aloud to Molly, I could see her struggling to commit them to memory.

THIS *ISN'T* A RECIPE.

WELL? WHAT *IS IT?!*

THE SWEETBERRY-BLOSSOM ONES WILL GIVE YOU CALM DREAMS.

I VERY MUCH ENJOY THEM, AND I THINK YOU WILL, TOO.

GOOD-BYE, NEWBOY.

NOSEGAY. I NEVER KNEW SHE CALLED ME THAT. NOSEBLEED, THEY CALLED ME ON THE STREETS.

I SUPPOSE THE OLDER ONES WHO KNEW WHAT NAME SHE HAD GIVEN ME THOUGHT IT WAS FUNNY.

AND AFTER A WHILE THEY PROBABLY FORGOT IT HAD EVER BEEN ANYTHING ELSE.

WELL, I DON'T CARE. I HAVE IT NOW. A NAME FROM MY MOTHER.

IT SUITS YOU.

THUD THUD THUD THUD

THUD THUD THUD THUD THUD THUD

BURRICH WILL HAVE *FITS* IF YOU BREAK THAT COLT'S KNEES!

NO!

HAH, YOU THOUGHT HE WAS A GHOST, SAME AS I.

YOU GAVE US A TURN, LAD. *APPEARING* LIKE THAT, LOOKING SO MUCH LIKE HIM. EY, REGAL?

VERITY, YOU'RE A FOOL. HOLD YOUR TONGUE.

WHAT *ARE* YOU DOING OUT ON THIS ROAD SO LATE, *BASTARD?*

JUST WHAT DO YOU THINK YOU'RE UP TO, *SNEAKING* AWAY FROM THE KEEP AND INTO TOWN AT THIS HOUR?

I'M ON MY WAY *BACK*, NOT *TO*, SIR.

I'VE BEEN RUNNING ERRANDS FOR FEDWREN.

OF *COURSE* YOU HAVE. SUCH A *LIKELY* TALE.

IT'S A BIT *TOO MUCH* OF A COINCIDENCE, BASTARD.

DON'T MIND HIM, BOY. YOU GAVE US *BOTH* A BIT OF A TURN.

A RIVER SHIP JUST CAME INTO TOWN, FLYING THE PENNANT FOR A *SPECIAL MESSAGE.*

AND WHEN REGAL AND I RODE DOWN TO GET IT, LO AND BEHOLD, IT'S FROM *PATIENCE...*

...TO TELL US CHIVALRY'S *DEAD.*

YOU ARE *SUCH* AN IDIOT, VERITY. TRUMPET IT OUT FOR THE *WHOLE TOWN* TO HEAR, BEFORE THE KING'S EVEN BEEN TOLD.

AND *DON'T* PUT IDEAS IN THE BASTARD'S HEAD THAT HE LOOKS LIKE CHIVALRY.

FROM WHAT *I* HEAR, HE HAS IDEAS *ENOUGH*. AND WE CAN THANK OUR *DEAR FATHER* FOR THAT.

COME *ON*. WE'VE GOT A MESSAGE TO DELIVER.

MY FATHER'S DEAD.

YES. MY BROTHER'S DEAD.

He granted me that, my uncle, that instant of kinship.

I think that ever after it changed how I saw the man.

UP BEHIND ME, BOY, AND I'LL TAKE YOU BACK TO THE KEEP.

NO, *THANK YOU.* BURRICH WOULD TAKE MY HIDE OFF FOR RIDING A HORSE DOUBLE ON THIS ROAD.

THAT HE *WOULD.*

I'M *SORRY* YOU FOUND OUT THIS WAY. I WASN'T THINKING.

IT... DOES NOT SEEM IT CAN BE *REAL.*

BUT *WHY SHOULD* I MOURN HIM? I DIDN'T EVEN *KNOW* HIM.

HE GOT ME ON SOME WOMAN. WHEN HE FOUND OUT ABOUT ME, HE *LEFT.* HE *NEVER CARED* ABOUT ME.

WHEN YOU ARE A MAN, MAYBE YOU'LL UNDERSTAND JUST *HOW MUCH* THAT COST HIM.

TO NOT KNOW YOU IN ORDER TO KEEP YOU *SAFE.* TO MAKE HIS ENEMIES *IGNORE* YOU.

HOW *WOULD YOU KNOW* HOW HE FELT?

IF *YOU* HAD KNOWN HE'D CARED, SO WOULD OTHERS.

"I KNEW HIM ALL HIS LIFE. I... WORKED WITH HIM. *MANY* TIMES.

"HAND IN GLOVE, AS THE SAYING GOES. AND I WAS THE *HAND.*

"THE HAND THAT MOVES UNSEEN, CLOAKED BY THE VELVET GLOVE OF *DIPLOMACY.*"

WHAT DO YOU *MEAN?*

THINGS CAN BE DONE. THINGS THAT MAKE DIPLOMACY... *EASIER.* OR A PARTY *MORE WILLING* TO NEGOTIATE. THINGS CAN *HAPPEN...*

A cold horror shook me as all the pieces suddenly fell into place.

All the lessons and careful instructions, the fullness of what Chade was and what I was to be.

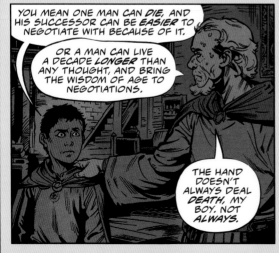

YOU MEAN ONE MAN CAN *DIE,* AND HIS SUCCESSOR CAN BE *EASIER* TO NEGOTIATE WITH BECAUSE OF IT.

OR A MAN CAN LIVE A DECADE *LONGER* THAN ANY THOUGHT, AND BRING THE WISDOM OF AGE TO NEGOTIATIONS.

THE HAND DOESN'T ALWAYS DEAL *DEATH,* MY BOY. NOT *ALWAYS.*

OFTEN *ENOUGH.*

I *NEVER* LIED TO YOU ABOUT THAT.

I THINK I'M GOING TO GO TO SHREWD AND TELL HIM TO FIND SOMEONE ELSE TO KILL PEOPLE FOR HIM.

THAT IS YOUR DECISION TO MAKE. BUT I ADVISE YOU AGAINST IT, FOR NOW.

WHY?

BECAUSE SOME WILL WANT TO WRITE FINIS TO CHIVALRY'S STORY. AND THAT WOULD BE BEST DONE BY ELIMINATING YOU.

THOSE ONES WILL BE WATCHING HOW YOU REACT TO YOUR FATHER'S DEATH. WILL YOU BECOME A PROBLEM NOW, THE WAY HE WAS?

HOW DID MY FATHER DIE?

THEY SAY HE FELL FROM A HORSE. BUT BURRICH SAID THAT CHIVALRY WOULD NOT FALL, NOR WOULD THAT HORSE THROW HIM.

I DON'T KNOW. BUT LIKE BURRICH, I DO NOT BELIEVE HE FELL FROM A HORSE.

ARE THEY GOING TO KILL ME, TOO?

I DON'T KNOW, NOT IF I CAN HELP IT. I THINK THEY MUST FIRST CONVINCE KING SHREWD IT IS NECESSARY.

AND IF THEY DO THAT, I SHALL KNOW OF IT.

THEN YOU THINK IT COMES FROM WITHIN THE KEEP.

I DO. BUT I KNEW NOTHING OF IT BEFORE IT HAPPENED. I HAD NO HAND IN IT.

THEY DIDN'T EVEN APPROACH ME. PROBABLY BECAUSE THEY KNOW I WOULD SEE THAT IT NEVER HAPPENED.

THEN THEY PROBABLY WON'T COME TO YOU IF THEY WANT ME DONE. THEY'D BE AFRAID OF YOUR WARNING ME.

YOUR FATHER'S DEATH SHOULD BE ALL THE WARNING YOU NEED. YOU'RE A BASTARD, BOY. WE'RE ALWAYS A RISK AND A VULNERABILITY.

HOLD THIS LESSON CLOSEST. IF EVER YOU MAKE IT SO THEY DON'T NEED YOU, THEY WILL KILL YOU.

FOR NOW, WE ARE THE **KING'S**. HIS **EXCLUSIVELY**, IN A WAY PERHAPS YOU HAVE NOT THOUGHT ABOUT.

NO ONE KNOWS WHAT I DO AND MOST HAVE FORGOTTEN WHO I AM. OR **WAS**. IF ANY KNOW OF US, IT IS FROM THE KING.

YOU SAID IT CAME FROM **WITHIN** THE KEEP. BUT IF YOU WERE **NOT** USED, THEN IT WAS **NOT** FROM THE KING...

THE QUEEN!

THAT'S A **DANGEROUS** ASSUMPTION TO MAKE. EVEN MORE DANGEROUS IF YOU THINK YOU MUST **ACT** ON IT.

WHY?

I HAVE NO **EVIDENCE** YOUR FATHER'S DEATH WAS THE QUEEN'S HAND STRIKING.

WHEN YOU SPRING TO AN IDEA, AND DECIDE IT IS TRUTH **WITHOUT** EVIDENCE, YOU BLIND YOURSELF TO OTHER POSSIBILITIES...

That is all I remember of our conversation then.

But I am sure that Chade had deliberately led me to consider who might have acted against my father.

And to instill in me a greater wariness of the Queen...

END OF PART ONE

Assassin's Apprentice

Sketchbook

Commentary by
Ryan Kelly

FITZ

Fitz's character design is pretty straightforward, and the only art direction I recall receiving outside of the prose novel text itself is that he should have "dark eyes." I didn't want to do anything radical or reinventive with Fitz, knowing that there is opportunity for growth in his appearance and manner throughout the story. I tended to extract Prince Chivalry and King Shrewd's look from him. Burrich, on the other hand, has a distinctive look all his own, and I feel proud that I designed a character that is intriguing and never boring to draw, even with the many scenes he shares with Fitz. Rugged, resourceful, loyal: these are the characteristics I ascribed to Burrich.

Assassin's Apprentice
BURRICH

ASSASSINS APPRENTICE
VERITY

Verity's design is one that was only discovered through the later process of story pages. I feel characters become their true selves in the panels and not in a single preliminary sketch. From my reading, Verity was "stocky" and not as refined as Chivalry. I ventured to design a prince that was always burdened with duties but could effortlessly produce a compassionate smile as well. After the sketch, his hair was properly lengthened and braided.

RYAN KELLY 2021

ASSASSINS APPRENTICE
REGAL

I tried to give Regal sharper features to match his personality, as well as present him with a full ensemble of fancy clothes adorned with gleaming gold and silver trinkets. I'm always searching for ways to give characters unique features to separate them, especially with a large cast, and that's why I initially drew Regal with light hair. Thankfully, we corrected that mistake in the story pages. I took the same approach with Hod. Drawing the Fool is difficult because the Fool is described as almost ageless or timeless in the book . . . A character I can't quite grasp when it comes to thoughts or emotions. A mysterious friend.

HOD
Assassin's Apprentice

FOOL
Assassin's Apprentice

In a way, every page is drawn four times: I design a small thumbnail shot of the page, then I draw a very rough layout in markers (not shown here) that I use as a basis for the actual penciled page, then I ink those pencils. Thus, I spend a lot of time on each page. But it gives me the chance to get the character acting just right as well as craft all the background details that make it feel like a real lived-in space.

A

Below are concepts for the first issue's cover from Anna Steinbauer. We knew we wanted an iconic image of Fitz here, so B was the choice. Anna produced an absolutely stellar cover, shown on the following page.

—Brett Israel (editor)

B

C

Assassin's Apprentice

will return

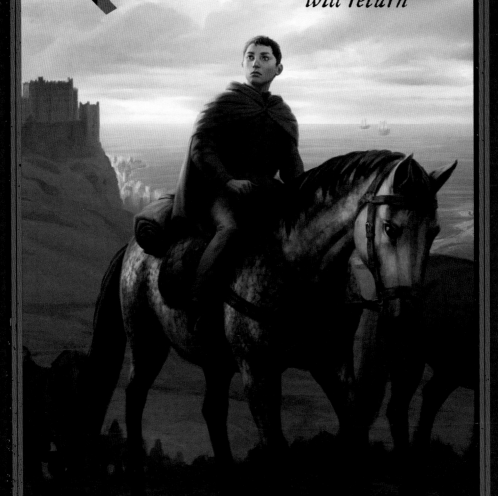